D1373144

DARK MAN

THE DARK SIDE OF MAGIC

by Peter Lancett

illustrated by Jan Pedroietta

SADDLEBACK
EDUCATIONAL PUBLISHING

DARK MAN

Blue Series

The Dark Fire of Doom
Destiny in the Dark
The Face in the Dark Mirror

The Dark Never Hides
Escape from the Dark
Fear in the Dark

Orange Series

Danger in the Dark
The Dark Dreams
The Dark Glass

The Dark Side of Magic
The Dark Waters of Time
The Shadow in the Dark

Green Series

The Dark Candle
The Dark Machine
The Dark Words

The Day Is Dark
Dying for the Dark
Killer in the Dark

Yellow Series

The Bridge of Dark Tears
The Dark Garden
The Dark Music

The Dark River
The Past Is Dark
Playing the Dark Game

© Ransom Publishing Ltd. 2007

Texts © Peter Lancett 2007

Illustrations © Jan Pedroietta 2007

David Strachan, The Old Man and The Shadow Masters appear
by kind permission of Peter Lancett

This edition is published by arrangement with Ransom Publishing Ltd.

SADDLEBACK
EDUCATIONAL PUBLISHING
www.sdlback.com

ISBN-13: 978-1-61651-019-0
ISBN-10: 1-61651-019-6
eBook: 978-1-63078-447-8

Printed in the U.S.A.

20 19 18 17 16   7 8 9 10 11

Chapter One:
The Girl Knows Magic

The Dark Man follows a girl.

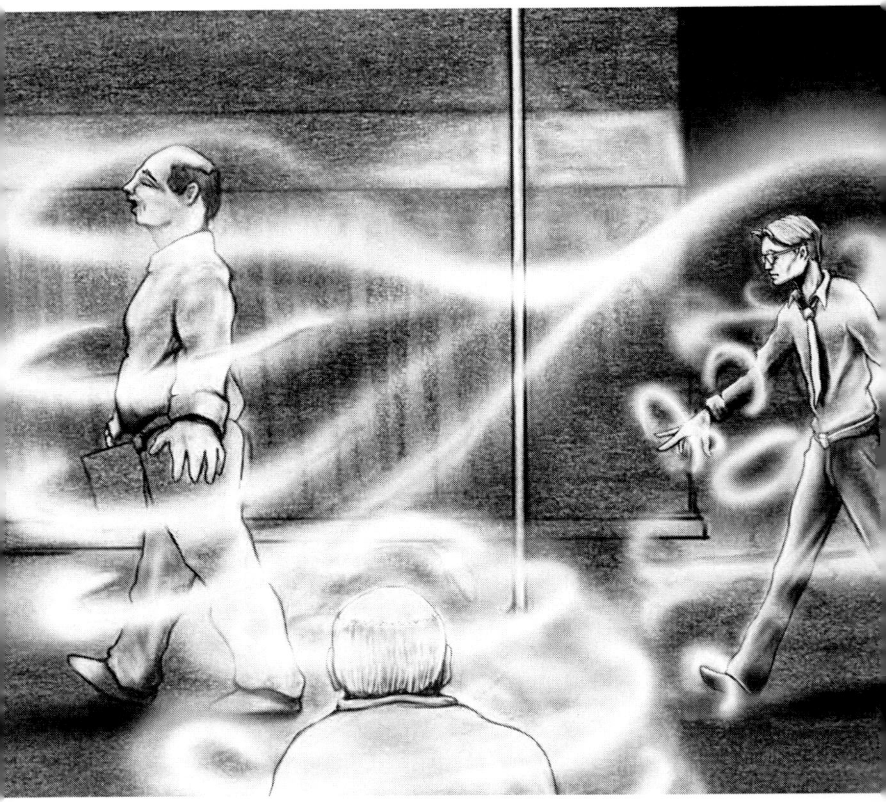

They are in the good part of the city.

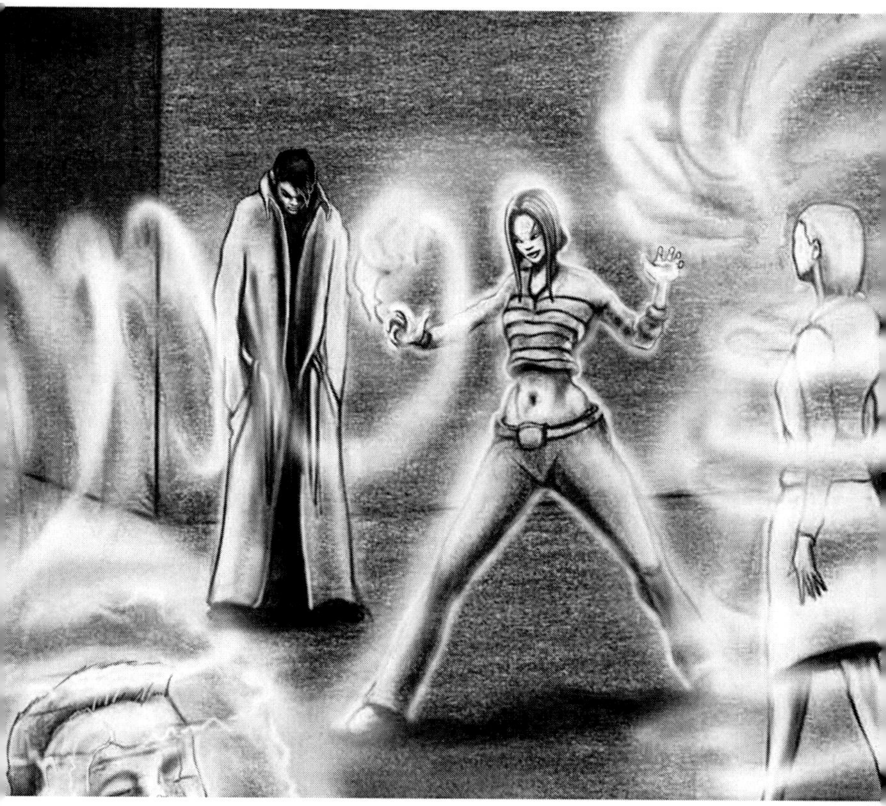

He sees her freeze time.

As the people stand still like statues, she steals from them.

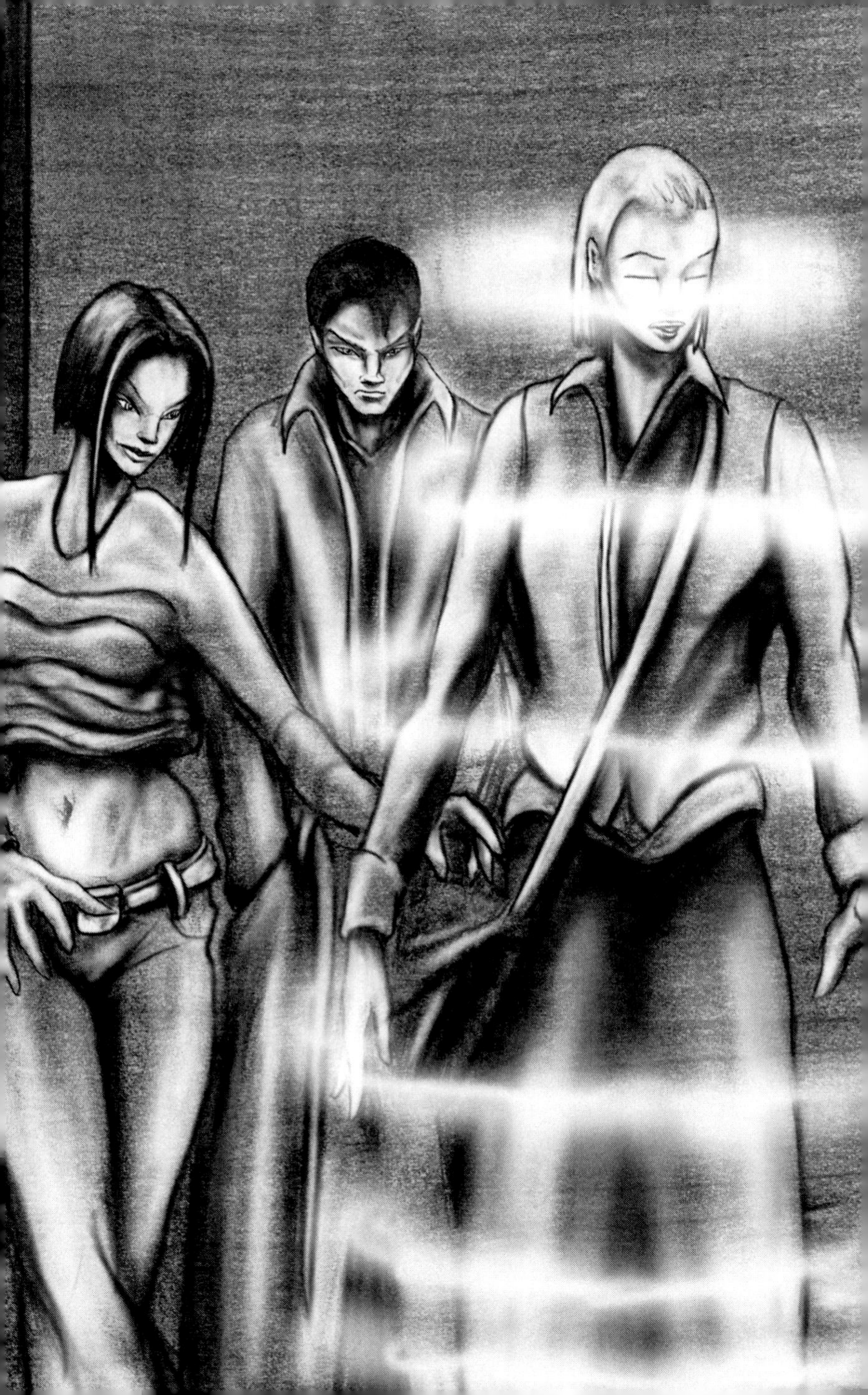

The Dark Man is not frozen.

He knows magic too.

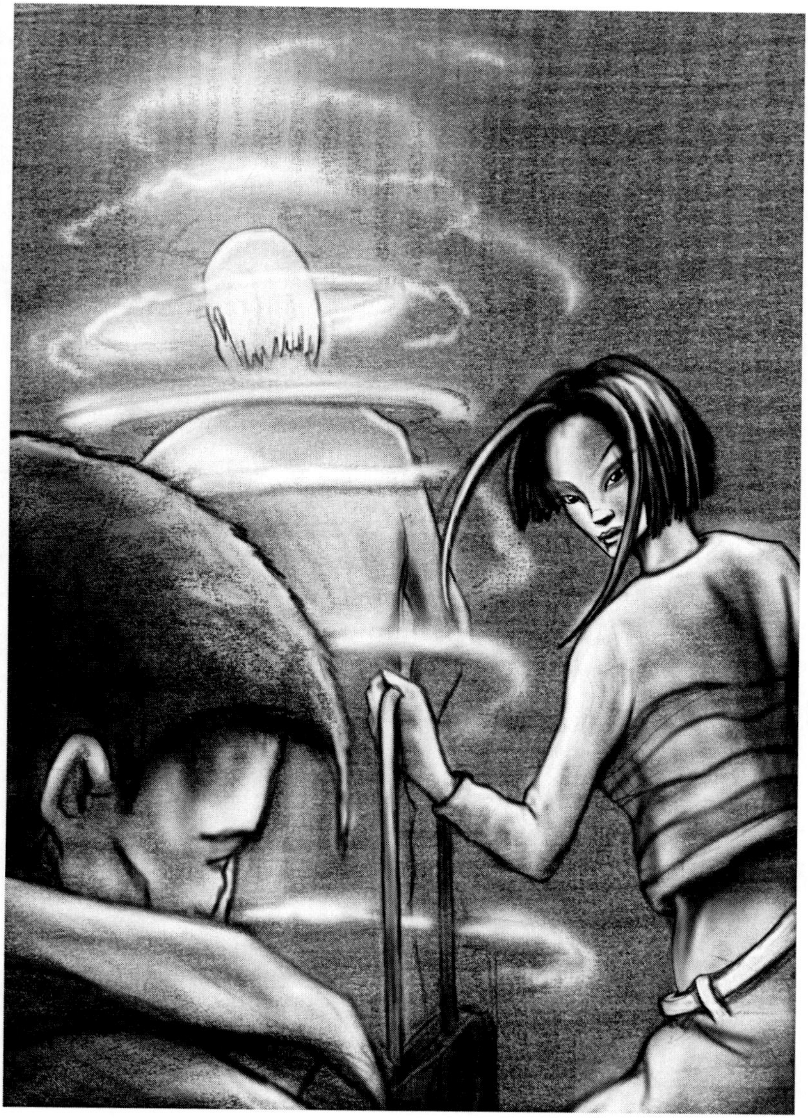

The girl turns and she sees the Dark Man.

It seems as if lights flash before his eyes.

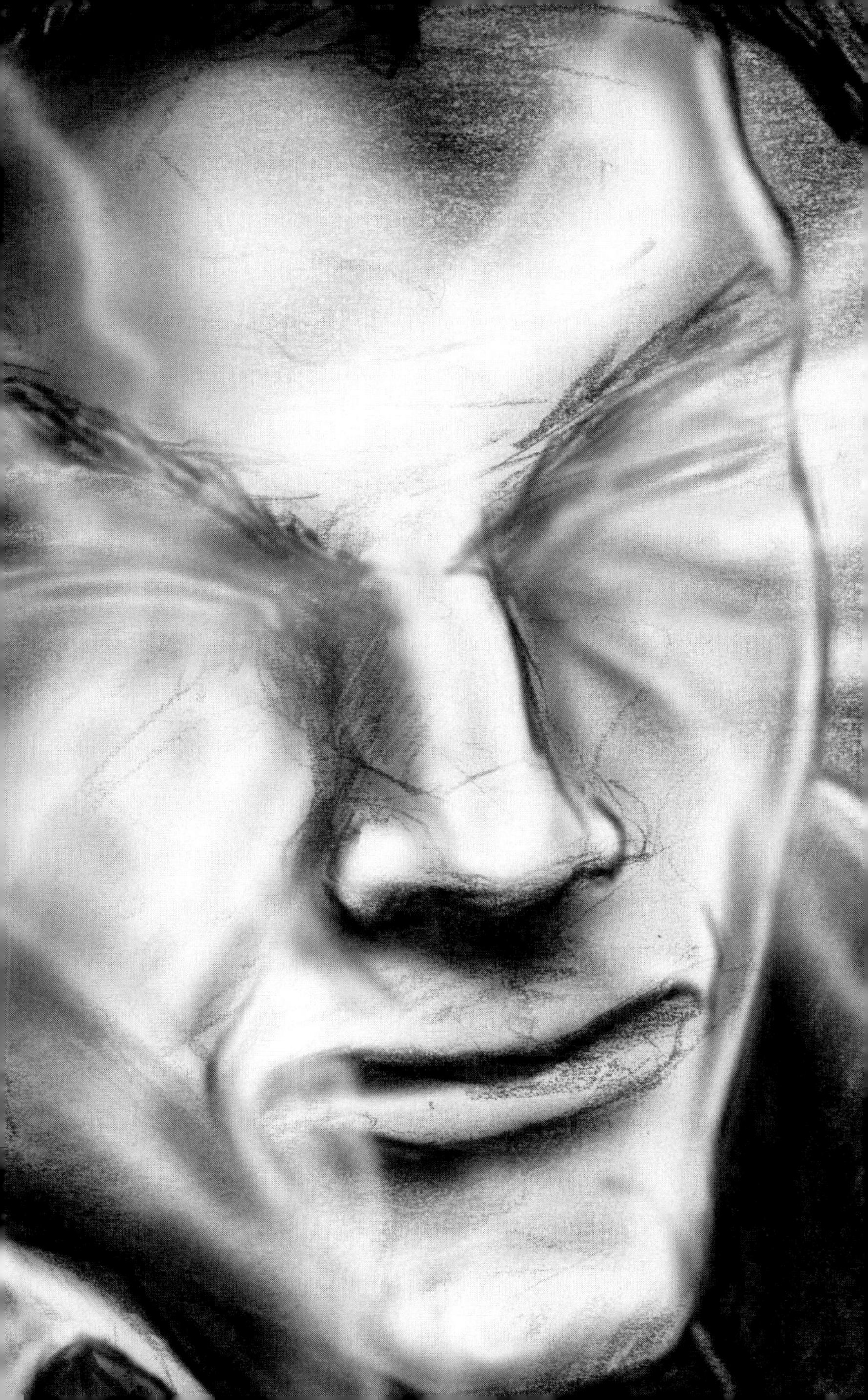

Then he finds himself in a stylish apartment.

Chapter Two:
Strong Powers

The girl stands before him.

"Did the Old Man send you?" she asks.

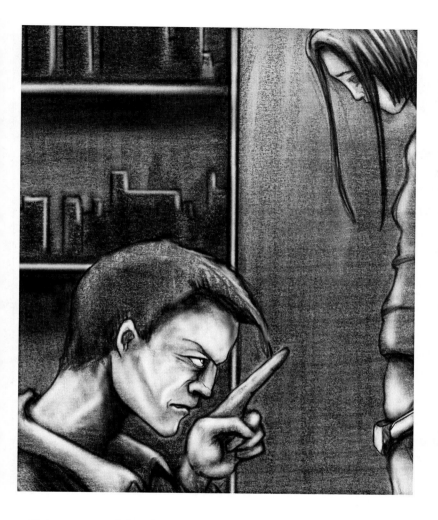

"He cares. He does not want bad things to happen to you."

"What could happen? I have strong powers.

"The Old Man asks me to use them and I help him."

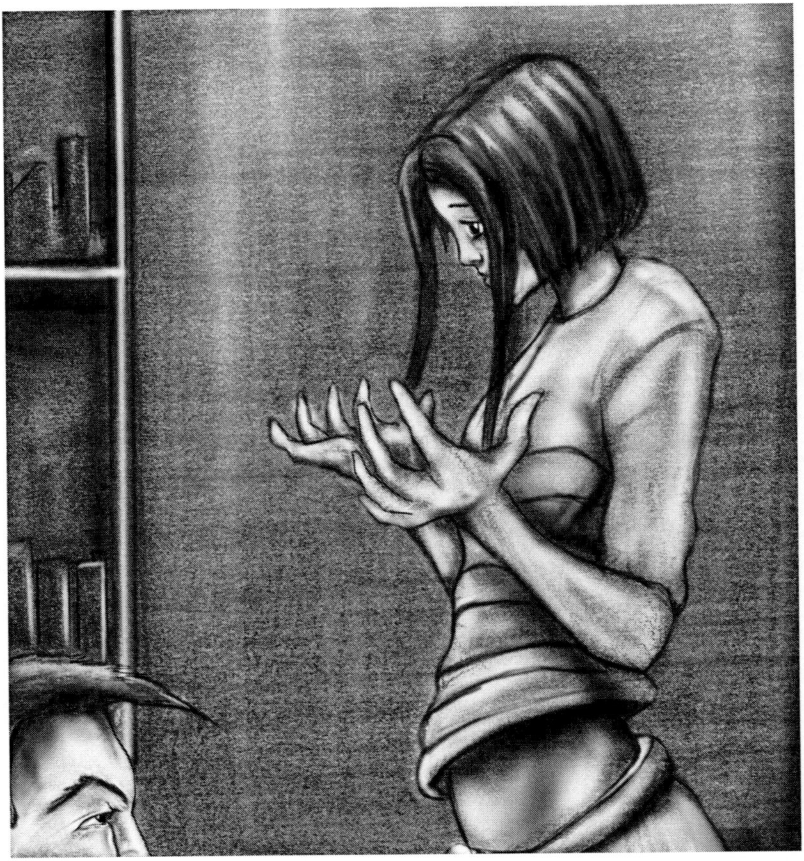

The Dark Man agrees.

"You must learn to control the magic or it will start to control you."

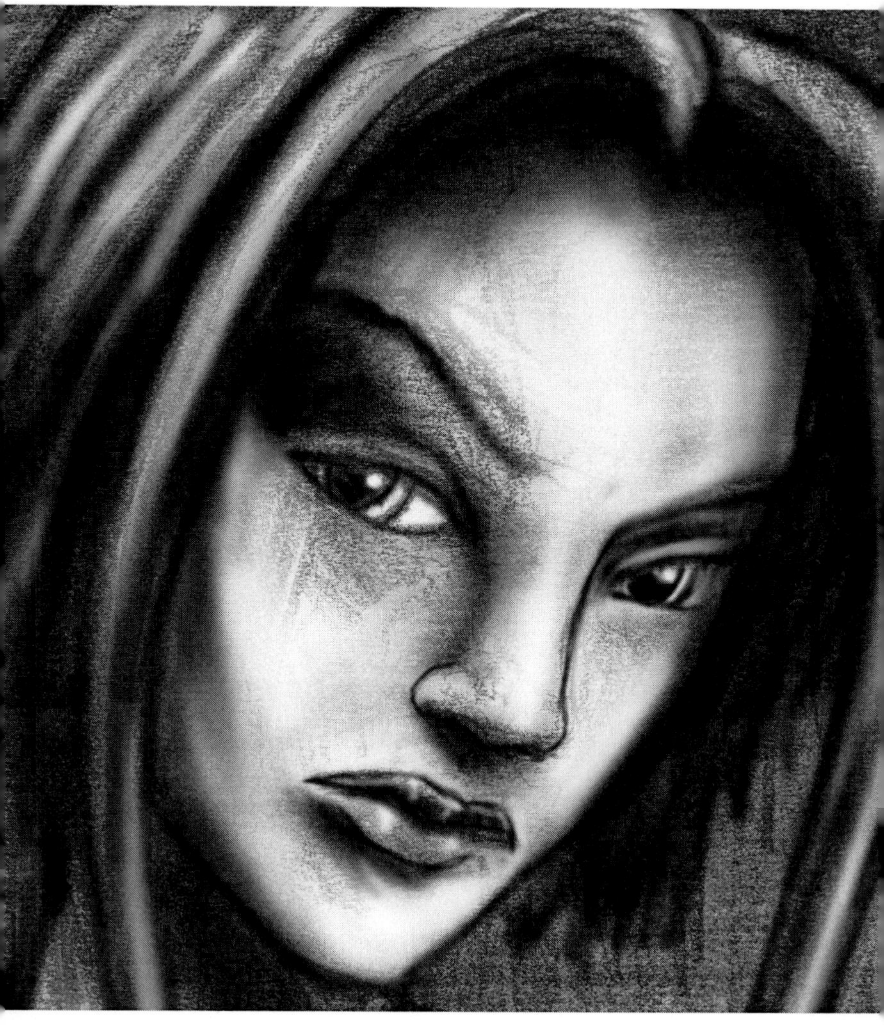

The girl shakes her head.

"Even the Shadow Masters cannot control me," she says.

Chapter Three:
Something Slimy

The Dark Man turns his head sharply.

Something slimy slithers back into a dark room.

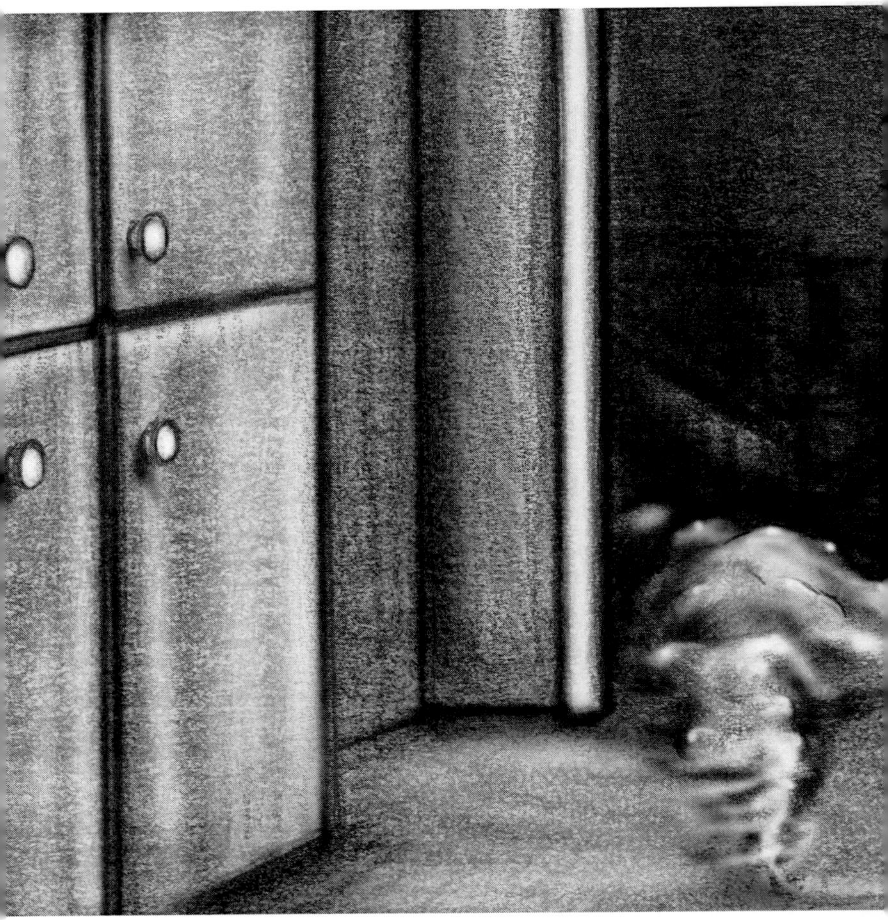

The girl smiles.

"Just my pet," she says.

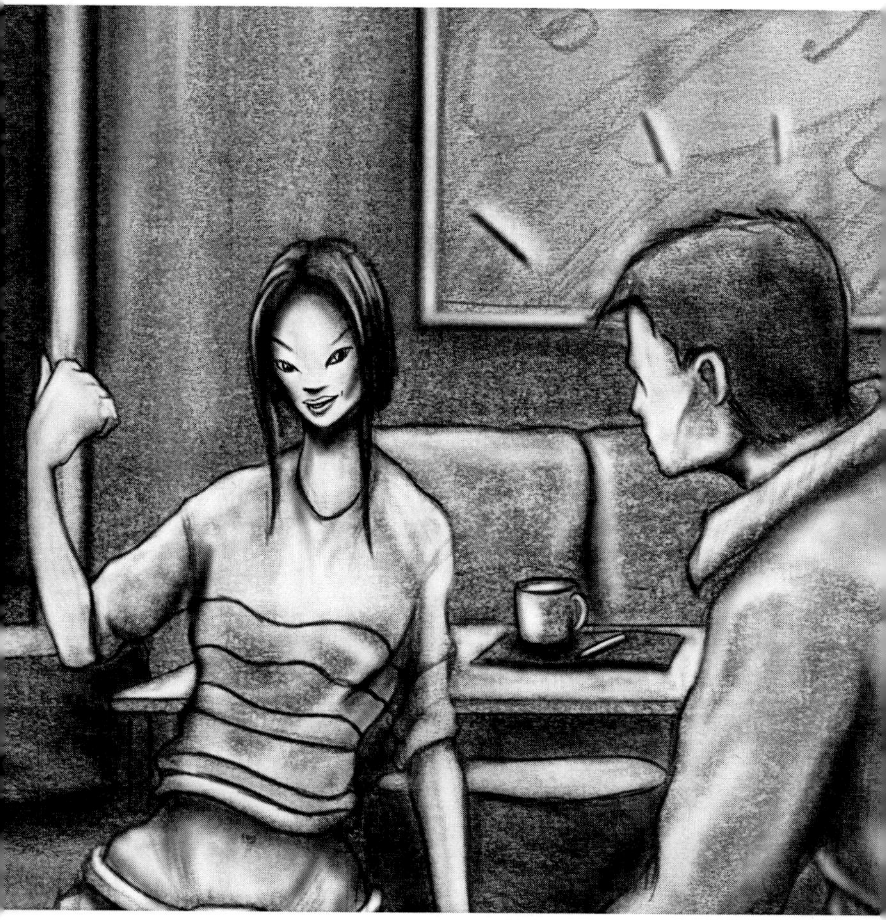

"Go to see the Old Man," the Dark Man says.

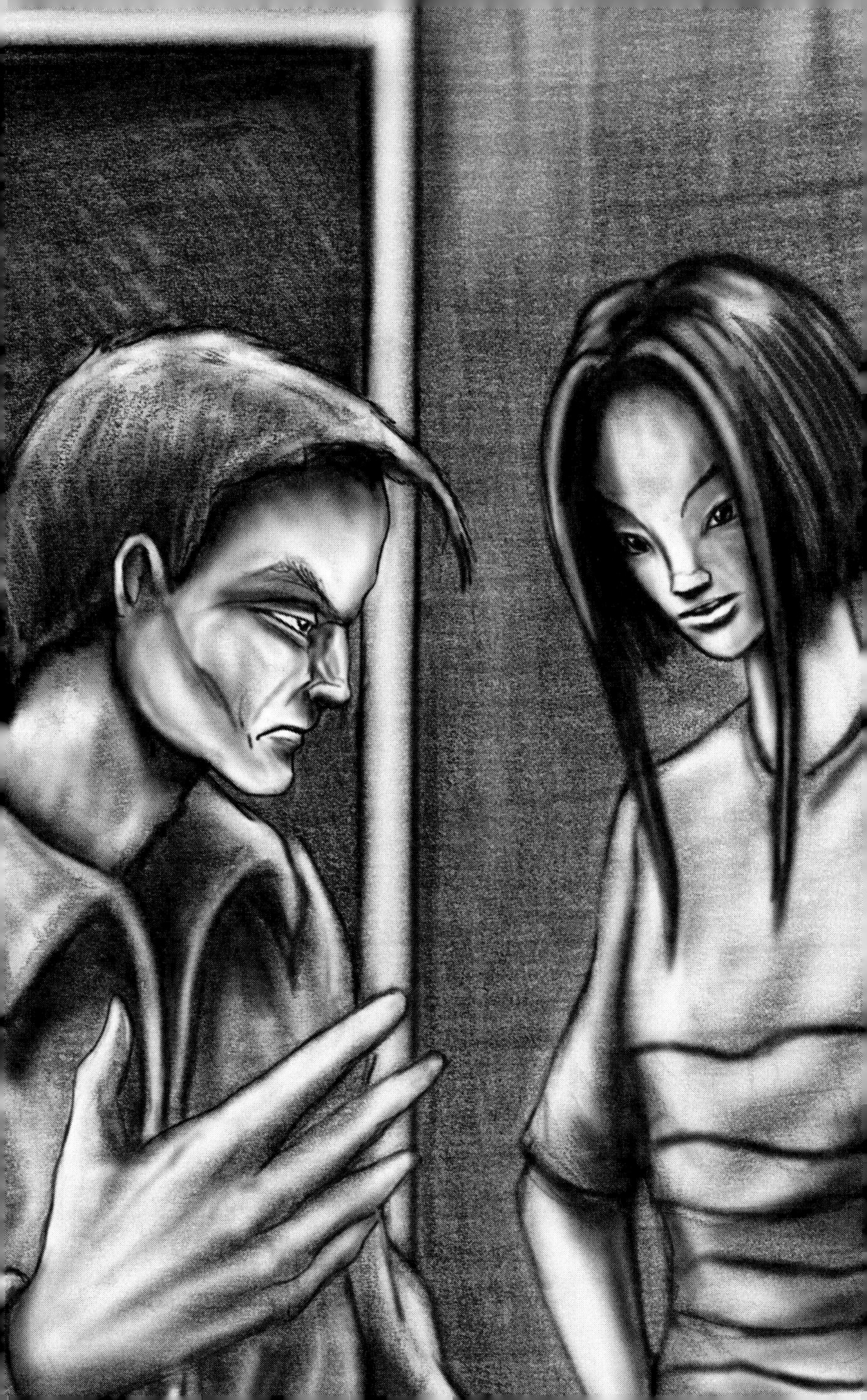

The slimy thing leaps out of the dark room.

The Dark Man turns to fight it.

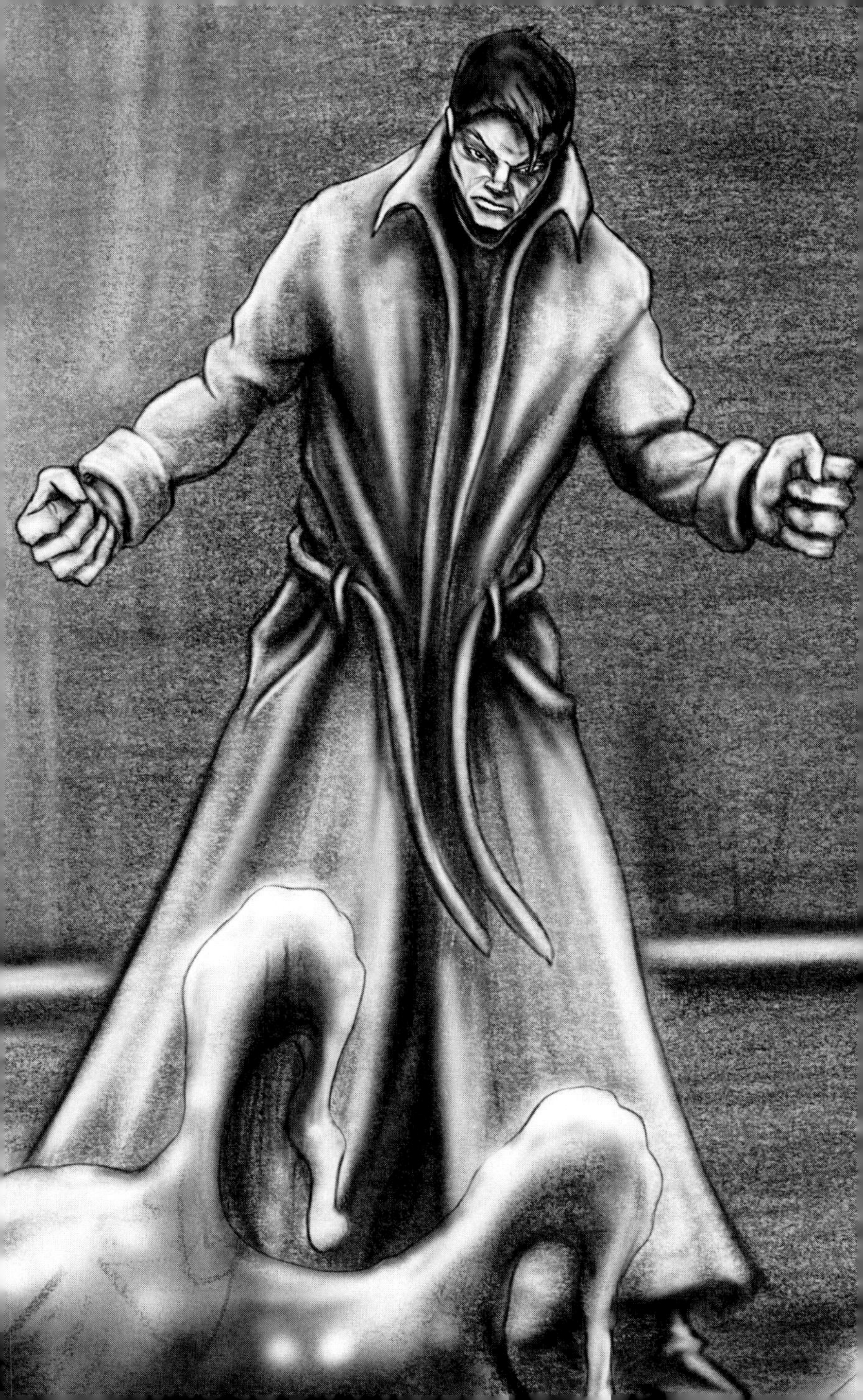

Chapter Four: On the Streets

But there is a flash of darkness and he finds himself back on the streets.

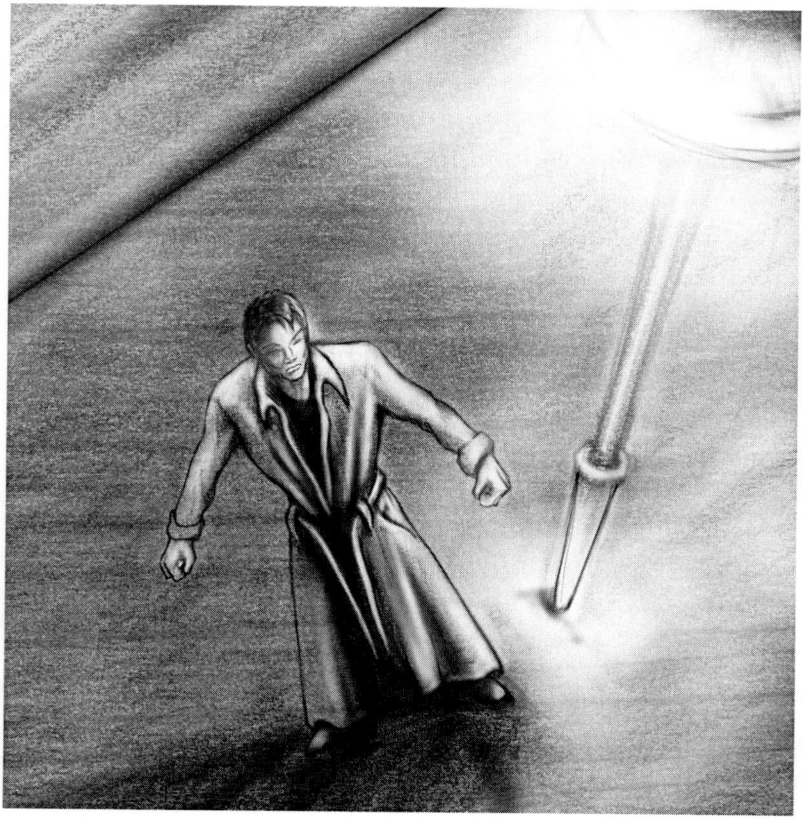

He shakes his head.

The Old Man must find the girl now.

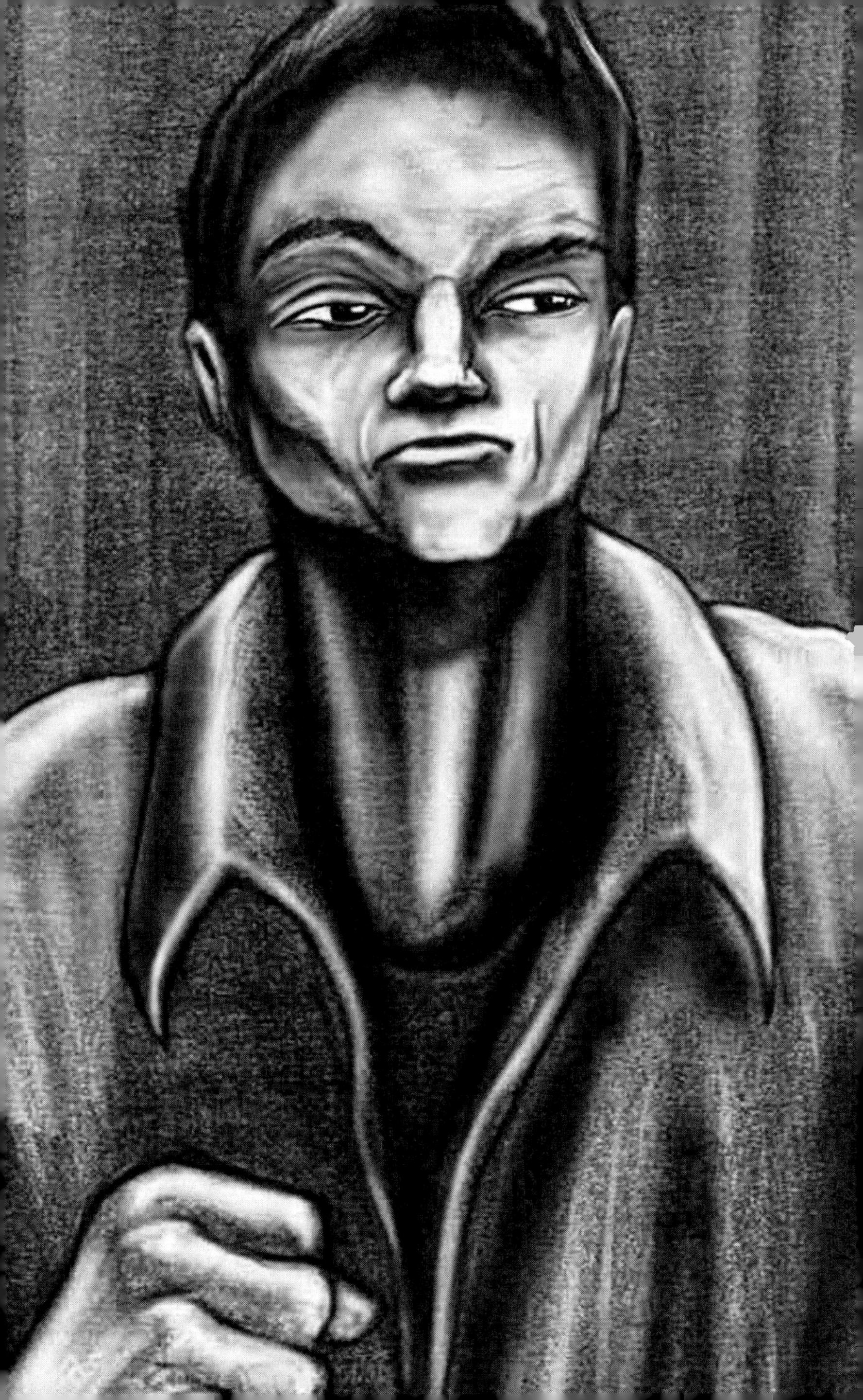

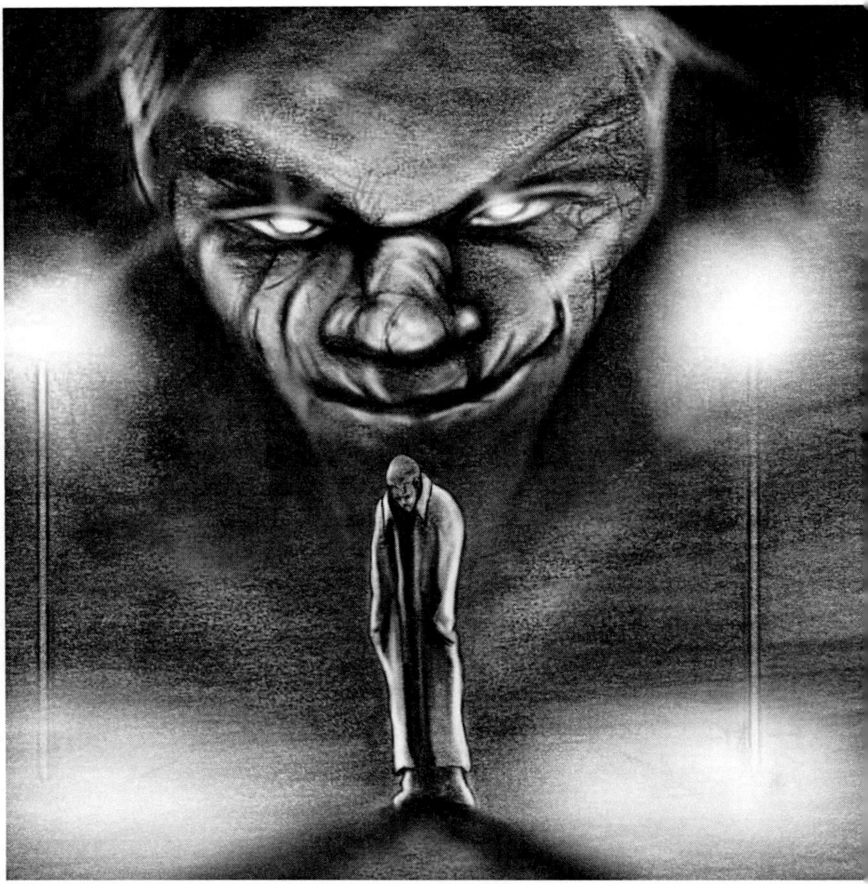

He hopes that he will not be too late.

THE AUTHOR

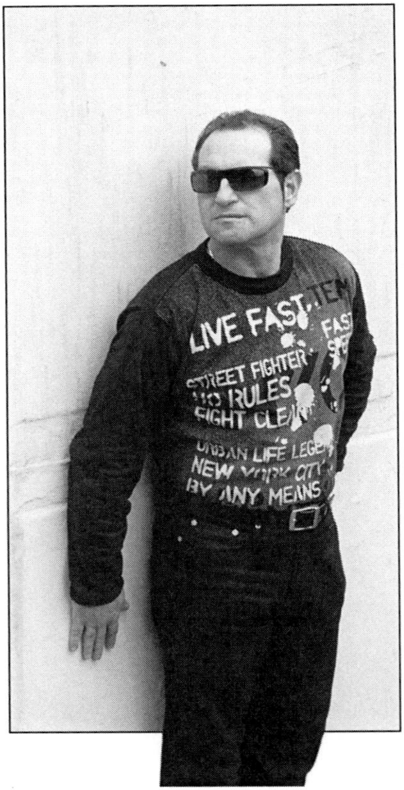
LIVE FAST
RULES
ANY MEANS

photograph: Rachel Ottewill

Peter Lancett used to work in the movies. Then he worked in the city. Now he writes horror stories for a living. "It beats having a proper job," he says.